characters created by
lauren child

I am really,
REALLY
Concentrating

PUFFIN

Text based on the script written by Samantha Hill

Illustrations from the TV animation produced by Tiger Aspect

PUFFIN BOOKS
Published by the Penguin Group: London, New York, Australia,
Canada, India, Ireland, New Zealand and South Africa
Penguin Books Ltd, Registered Offices: 80 Strand, London WC2R 0RL, England

puffinbooks.com

This edition published in Great Britain in Puffin Books 2012
001 – 10 9 8 7 6 5 4 3 2 1
Text and illustrations copyright © Lauren Child/Tiger Aspect Productions Limited, 2008
Charlie and Lola word and logo ® and © Lauren Child, 2005
Charlie and Lola is produced by Tiger Aspect Productions
All rights reserved
The moral right of the author/illustrator has been asserted
Manufactured in China
ISBN: 978-0-718-19530-4
This edition produced for the Book People Ltd,
Hall Wood Avenue, Haydock, St Helens, WA11 9UL

I have this little sister Lola.
She is small and very funny.
          Lola is very excited because
it's almost Sports Day. And this is Lola's
          first ever Sports Day.

Lola says,
"What do you do on Sports Day?"

And I say,
"There are all sorts of races... like running."

"I don't like running."

So I say, "There's also **jumping**."

"Not **jumping**, Charlie. My legs are quite short."

Then I say, "Let's go to the park
to practise some **games** with
Lotta and Marv."

At the park, I say,
     "Let's try the **three-legged** race."

Lola says,
     "That sounds ᴇᵃˢʸ-ᵖᵉᵃˢʸ!"

"Easy-peasy lemon-squeezy!" says Lotta.

Then I say,
  "Maybe we should try the **obstacle** race?"

"Oc-to-pus race?" says Lola.

You **run** twice round the boot,
   skip twice with the **skipping** rope,
do two circles with the hula hoops,
  and **bounce** the ball on the racket.

On your marks, **get set, GO!**"

Lotta crosses the finish line first.
But Lola is a bit more slow.

Lotta says, "I think the
oc-to-pus race is the very best!"

Marv says,
"Well done, Lotta.
You'll be really good at Sports Day.
But what about Lola?"

Later, Lola says,
"I still don't know what **race** to do."

And I say, "I know!
The **egg**-and-**spoon** race!"

Lola says, "Yes! Because I love **eggs**
and I love **spoons**!

Charlie, what is the **egg**-and-**spoon** race?"

I say, "It's when you run a race
balancing an **egg** on a spoon."

So Lola practises...
and practises...
and soon she says...

"Look, Charlie!
I am a champion egg-and-spooner!"

So I say, "Lola, did you glue
the **egg** to the **spoon**?"

"Yes, Charlie. Now it doesn't fall off!"

"But Lola, that's **cheating**."

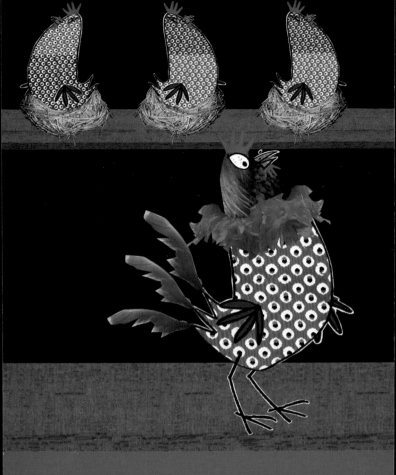

"Then I need to find an **egg**
                    that's not all **wobbly**.
A perfect **egg**, from a perfect chicken,
                    that I will never EVER drop."

I say, "But it's OK to **drop** it. You just have to put it back on the **spoon** and keep going."

But Lola says, "No, Charlie. I do not want to drop this **egg** because it is completely perfect."

Later, Lola says,
        "Oh, I'm NEVER going to get the
egg to stay on my **SpoOn**."

So I say,
        "You will! You just have to **concentrate**.

Don't take your eyes off it for one single second. Do you understand?"

Lola says,
"Oh, I can **Con-cen-trate**.
I know I can, Charlie."

At Sports Day me and Marv
    do the **three-legged** race.

Lotta does the **obstacle** race,
    and then it's Lola's turn.

I shout,
"CONCENTRATE, Lola!"

Marv shouts,
"You can do it, Lola!"

Then Lotta says,
        "She's not going very **fast**, is she?"

And I say,
        "Oh dear...
                she is last."

But, after the race, Lola says,
"Look! Mrs Hanson gave me an
ever-so-special ribbon because
my **egg** did not fall off my **spoon**
even **one single** time!"